A Break-of-Day Book®

Ever since 1928, when Wanda Gág's classic *Millions of Cats* appeared, Coward, McCann & Geoghegan has been publishing books of high quality for young readers. Among them are the easy-to-read stories known as Break-of-Day books. This series appears under the colophon shown above— a rooster crowing in the sunrise—which is adapted from one of Wanda Gág's illustrations for *Tales from Grimm*.

Though the language used in Break-of-Day books is deliberately kept as clear and as simple as possible, the stories are not written in a controlled vocabulary. And while chosen to be within the grasp of readers in the primary grades, their content is far-ranging and varied enough to captivate children who have just begun crossing the momentous threshold into the world of books.

Coward, McCann & Geoghegan, Inc.
New York

The
Scariest
Witch in
Wellington
Towers

by Joyce Segal
pictures by Margot Apple

LIBRARY OF CONGRESS CATALOGING IN PUBLICATION DATA
Segal, Joyce.
  The scariest witch in Wellington Towers.
  SUMMARY: Bonny's Halloween round as the scariest
witch in her apartment building has a surprise ending.
  [1. Halloween—Fiction. 2. Apartment houses—
Fiction] I. Apple, Margot. II. Title.
PZ7.S4526c [Fic] 79-12239
ISBN 0-698-30722-4

First printing
Printed in the United States of America

for Mathilda, Florence, and Ruth...
my favorite witches
J. S.

It was Halloween.
Bonny put on her
pointed black hat,
her big black cape,
and her witch's mask.   9

"Boo!" she said.

"Now I'm not Bonny anymore.

Now I'm a witch."

"Mew!" said the cat.

He didn't look scared.

The Witch tiptoed

behind her mother's chair.

"Boo!" she said.

"Help!" said her mother.

"Who are you?"

She jumped out of her chair.   11

"I'm the scariest witch
in the world," said the Witch.
She used her shaky, scary voice.
"Ooh, I'm so scared
I can't stand it,"
said her mother.

The Witch giggled.

"Oh, Mommy," she said.

"You're not really scared.

You knew it was me.

But I'm going to scare

everybody else

in the whole world."

"All right," said her mother.
"But be sure to stay in
Wellington Towers."
"I will," said the Witch,
and she waved good-bye.

"Mew!" said the cat,
and he jumped onto
the Witch's shoulder.
The Witch tiptoed
down the hall.
There were colorful
Halloween pictures
on many of the apartment doors.
Living in Wellington Towers
was fun.
There were halls to run in
and elevators to ride in.
There were babies and baby sitters,
and cats and dogs.

There were lots of boys, too.

They were all right.

But there were no other girls

the right age to play with.

The Witch went to a door

with a pumpkin picture.

She rang the bell

and the door opened.

"Boo!" said the Witch.

"Mew!" said the cat.

"My goodness!" said Mrs. Baker.

"What a scary witch!"

"Mew!" said the cat again.

"And the cat is scary, too,"

said Mrs. Baker.

"Hmm, I wonder if the Witch
would like a lollipop."
"Thank you, Mrs. Baker,"
said the Witch.
"You're welcome, Witch,"
said Mrs. Baker.

The Witch tiptoed down the hall.

The cat tried to grab the lollipop.

The Witch went to a door

with a haunted house picture.

She rang the bell

and the door opened.

"Boo!" said the Witch.

"Mew!" said the cat.

"Who in the world are you?"
asked Mr. Clark.

"I'm a witch," said the Witch.

She used her scary voice.

"Can't you tell?"

"Just a minute," said Mr. Clark.

"You do sound scary,

but I'm afraid I can't see a thing

without my glasses."

He turned and called inside,

"Tilly, where are my glasses?"

A voice called back,

"Probably on your head,

where they always are!"

"She's right!" said Mr. Clark,

and he put on his glasses.

"And you're right!" he said.

"You are a witch.

As a matter of fact,
you're the scariest witch
I ever saw.
Maybe I'd better give you
a very big apple."
"Thank you, Mr. Clark,"
said the Witch.

"You're welcome, Bonny,"
said Mr. Clark.
The Witch tiptoed down the hall.
The cat tried to grab the apple.
The Witch rang for the elevator.
Out came the mailman.
"Boo!" said the Witch.

"Mew!" said the cat.

He jumped into the mailman's bag.

"Oh, hi, Bonny.

You scared me for a minute,"

said the mailman.

"I'm scaring everybody today,"

said the Witch.

"I'm not Bonny anymore.

I'm a witch."

"That's nice," said the mailman.

"Say, some new people

moved into Apartment 4C.

They have a girl about your age."

"Good. I'm going to scare her,"

said the Witch.   25

She didn't want him to know
how excited she was.
She waved good-bye
and got into the elevator.
The cat jumped out of
the mailman's bag
and got into the elevator, too.

"Did you hear that?"

said the Witch.

"A new girl!"

Now we'll really have some fun!"

"Mew!" said the cat.

There was a Monster
inside the elevator.
"You can't scare me,"
said the Monster.
"You can't scare me either,"
28   said the Witch.

The elevator went down.

When it stopped, a Ghost got in.

"You can't scare me,"
said the Monster.

"You can't scare me either,"
said the Ghost.

"You can't scare me either,"
said the Witch.

"And you can't even scare my cat."

TRICK
or
TREAT

now give
me some-
thing good
to eat.

The elevator went down.

When it stopped, a Skeleton got in.

"Yuck," said the Monster.

"Ugh," said the Ghost.

"Creep," said the Skeleton.

"Silly," said the Witch.

"Mew," said the cat.

The elevator went down
to the lobby.
The Monster, the Ghost,
and the Skeleton got out.
"Aren't you coming with us?"
asked the Monster.

"No thanks," said the Witch.

"I'm busy right now.

I'll see you later."

Everybody waved good-bye.

The Witch and the cat

were alone in the elevator.

They went up to the fourth floor.

The Witch tiptoed to Apartment 4A.

The cat crept behind the Witch.

The Witch rang the bell.

Mrs. Greenberg wasn't home.

The Witch tiptoed to Apartment 4B.

The cat crept behind the Witch.

The Witch rang the bell.

Miss Quinn wasn't home.

The Witch tiptoed to Apartment 4C.

The cat crept behind the Witch.

How quiet it was.

The hall was
very long and dark.

The Witch and the cat
were all alone.

Then the elevator door opened.

But nobody got out.

The Witch and the cat
were still all alone.

The hall was longer
and darker than before.

The ghost pictures looked real.

They looked ready to jump off the doors.

The Witch waved her arms.

She wanted to practice being scary before she rang a strange doorbell.

She waved her arms again.

She hunched up her shoulders.

There.

That was better.

That was really scary.

She took a deep breath
and rang the bell.
The cat jumped up

and tried to ring the bell, too.

The Witch could hear

the sound of feet running inside.

They were running toward the door.

She could hear a laugh.

It was a strange laugh.

It was a scary laugh.

"Mew!" said the cat.

He hid behind the Witch.

Maybe she should run!

But it was too late.

The Witch began to say, "Boo."

The door began to open.

Behind the door was...

another Witch!

"Help!" the Witch screamed.

"Help!" the other Witch screamed.

"Help!" the two Witches screamed
together.

"Mew!" said the cat.

He looked scared, too.

The Witches stopped screaming.

Slowly, they both took off their
masks
and peeked through their fingers.

They gave each other
tight little sideways smiles.
Then the smiles grew wider.
Now Wellington Towers
had two witches without front teeth!
The tight little sideways smiles
grew into big fat grins.
"I'm Bonny," said one Witch.
"I'm Nancy," said the other Witch.

"Mew!" said the cat.

He crept behind them

as they held hands

and tiptoed through the halls.   43

Two witches were
twice as much fun!
They were the Scariest Witches
in Wellington Towers!

BOO!

ABOUT THE AUTHOR

Joyce Segal was born in Brooklyn, New York, and was graduated from the City College of New York. After a career as an advertising copywriter she turned her writing talents to children's books. This is her second book for children. She lives in Teaneck, New Jersey, with her husband and daughter.

ABOUT THE ARTIST

Margot Apple was born in Detroit, Michigan, and graduated from New York's Pratt Institute with a BFA. While establishing herself as an illustrator, she worked at various jobs including cook and bus driver. She has illustrated over one dozen books. Ms. Apple has made New England her home for the past eight years.